OLD BLACK FLY

JIM AYLESWORTH

Illustrations by
STEPHEN GAMMELL

SCHOLASTIC INC.
New York Toronto London Auckland Sydney

To my brother Bill,
a legendary swatter of flies,
with love.   —J. A.

ISBN 0-590-46361-6

Text copyright © 1992 by Jim Aylesworth.
Illustrations copyright © 1992 by Stephen Gammell.
All rights reserved. Published by Scholastic Inc., 730 Broadway,
New York, NY 10003, by arrangement with Henry Holt and
Company, Inc.

12 11 10 9 8 7 6 5 4 3 2 1   3 4 5 6 7 8/9

Printed in the U.S.A.   08

First Scholastic printing, January 1993

Old black fly's been
buzzin' around,
buzzin' around,
buzzin' around.
Old black fly's been
buzzin' around,
And he's had a very
busy bad day.

He ate on the crust
of the **A**pple pie.

He bothered the Baby
and made her cry.
Shoo fly!
Shoo fly!
Shooo.

He coughed on the Cookies
with the chocolate bits.

He drove the **D**og
nearly out of his wits.
Shoo fly!
Shoo fly!
Shooo.

He frolicked on the **E**ggs
for the birthday cake.

He licked up the **F**rosting,
for goodness sake.
Shoo fly!
Shoo fly!
Shooo.

He danced on the edge
of the **G**arbage sack.

He got sweet **H**oney
on his dirty back.
Shoo fly!
Shoo fly!
Shooo.

He hid in the Ivy
by the kitchen sink.

He stole some **J**elly
as quick as a wink.
Shoo fly!
Shoo fly!
Shooo.

He played on the **K**eys
by the kitchen door.

He lit on the **L**ist
for the grocery store.
Shoo fly!
Shoo fly!
Shooo.

chocolate
eggs
apples
olive oil
honey
milk
salami
jelly
noodles

He lapped up the **M**ilk
in poor kitty's bowl.

He nibbled on **N**oodles
in the casserole.
Shoo fly!
Shoo fly!
Shooo.

He crawled in the spills
from the Olive oil can.

He pestered the **P**arrot
on her stand.
	Shoo fly!
	Shoo fly!
	Shooo.

He snoozed on the **Q**uilt
on Gramma's bed.

He rode the red **R**ibbon
on her head.
Shoo fly!
Shoo fly!
Shooo.

He sniffed the **S**alami
that sister sliced.

He ran around her Teacup
once or twice.
Shoo fly!
Shoo fly!
Shooo.

He slept on the stack
of clean Underwear.

He played on the **V**ase
by the velvet chair.
Shoo fly!
Shoo fly!
Shooo.

He dozed on the **W**indow
in the summer heat.

He made a little
with his front feet.
        Shoo fly!
        Shoo fly!
        Shooo.

He buzzed about the **Y**arn in Mama's lap.

He landed on her table,
flap flip flap.

Old black fly's done
buzzin' around,
buzzin' around,
buzzin' around.
Old black fly's done
buzzin' around,
and he won't be bad
no more.